D0683523

THE ADVENTURES OF TOM AND ANDY

BOOK I

The Legend of Black Eyed Bart

Edward Penner

For kids who like fast-paced,
exciting stories.

For kids who like action
and amazing adventures.

I wrote this book for you.

Table of Contents

Chapter 1:
Looks Like Rain

• • • • •

At last, the school day was over. Tom grabbed his Grade 2 reader and his math workbook. He stuffed them into his backpack. Then he reached up to grab his coat off the hook.

I've got to hurry, he thought to himself. *Andy will be waiting.* He had told his friend Andy that he would come over right after school.

Tom tossed his coat over his shoulder. He didn't want to wear it, even though it was a cool spring day. The sun hid behind dark clouds. It looked like rain, but so far none had fallen. If he got home fast, he would still have time to go bike riding.

He ran for the back door. Past his Grade 2 class and past the Grade 4 class.

Hmph, he thought. *That's Jason's class. I hope he's not around.*

Just then Tom heard the click-clack of his shoelaces bouncing on the ground. *Rats. I hate it when my shoes come untied.*

Tom reached down to tie his laces. He was almost finished when someone bumped him hard from behind. He fell forward, face down into the hallway. His backpack and his coat fell to the ground.

"Ha, ha, ha," came the laughter from behind him.

"Hey," he said turning around. "What's so funny?" Tom looked up to see a boy with bright red hair standing above him.

It was Jason. Beside Jason was his friend Kyle. Both of them were laughing.

"Learn to stand on your feet," said Jason. "Don't you know how to walk yet?" Jason turned to his friend Kyle. "These little kids can't do anything." The two boys kept laughing as they went down the hall.

Tom struggled to his feet.

"I'll show you," he called after them. "One day you will see what I can do." But it was too late. The two ruffians had already gone out the back door.

Tom saw someone waving to him down the hall. It was his best friend, Andy.

"Tom, come on. It's going to rain soon. We have to hurry."

Tom raced ahead to meet Andy. Andy grinned his big grin. He had a smile that could make anyone forget their troubles. Even if those troubles had the names Jason and Kyle.

"You ok?" asked Andy.

"I'm great," said Tom, grinning back. "Let's grab our bikes and go. I'll race you to my house. I know a special place where we can go riding today. A place where pirates lived!"

Chapter 2:
The Old Beemer House

• • • • •

Andy zoomed into Tom's driveway a split second before Tom.

"I win," said Andy.

"Rats," said Tom. "How come you always win?"

"That's easy," replied Andy. "I'm a year older than you."

"I wish I was eight," said Tom, standing on his tip toes. "Then I would be as tall as you. And you would have trouble beating me in a race."

"Well you are only seven." Andy grinned at his friend. "You can't change that. Where did you want to go riding today?"

"I've got the perfect spot," said Tom. "The old Beemer place."

"Beemer? There's nothing there," said Andy. "Just the old house. No one has lived there for ages."

"But a pirate used to live there," said Tom.

"No way!" Andy leaned forward, listening closely. "Beemer was a pirate?"

Tom laughed. "Not Beemer. Before the Beemers lived up on that hill a pirate used to live there. They called him Black Eyed Bart."

"Black Eyed Bart?" Andy was surprised. "I've never heard of him."

"Frank told me about him," said Tom.

Frank was Tom's older brother. He was eleven. He was studying history in his Grade 6 class. Frank's teacher, Mr. Niko, was a history expert. He knew all about pirates. He'd told Frank's class about Black Eyed Bart.

"It was a long time ago," said Tom. "Bart disappeared after a big fight on the hill."

"What happened?" asked Andy.

"No one knows exactly," replied Tom. "But a pirate did live there. Someone found musket balls there years ago. They are in the museum now. I want to try to find something too."

"Do you think we can?" Andy asked.

"Yup. Maybe we can find Black Eyed Bart's musket. No one has ever found it," said Tom.

"Cool. Let's go," said Andy excitedly.

"Great," said Tom. "Go tell your parents we are going out. I will tell mine too. We can meet in your driveway in five minutes."

Andy zoomed off to his house. Meanwhile, Tom bounded up the front steps. He raced inside to tell his mother he was going riding. She warned him about the weather.

"Don't get caught in the rain," she said. "There's a big storm coming. Maybe you should play inside."

"Not today," said Tom. "Andy and I are going out. I'll be back for supper."

"Ok, but be careful," she said.

Tom pedaled down the street. Andy's house was only four doors down. He always got there fast. As he pulled into the driveway, Andy came outside.

"All set," called Andy. "Let's go."

The two boys rode quickly down the street. There were never many cars here. Tom liked that. It made it easy for bike riding.

Soon they came to the bottom of Beemer's Hill. That's when the riding got hard. They huffed. They puffed. They rode as hard as they could. Finally, they reached the top of the hill.

"Let's rest," said Tom. "I'm tired."

"Me too," replied Andy. "How much farther to Beemer's place?"

"It's just over there," said Tom pointing. "Do you see that rickety old place?"

"Yes."

"That's it," said Tom. "Ready?"

"Race you there," said Andy.

Tom felt a wet drop land on his nose. Then another drop landed on his arm. A third drop landed on his ear. Then a whole lot of drops landed all over him.

"Hey, it's pouring," yelled Tom.

"Let's go for cover," cried Andy. "Over there. Under that tree."

The two boys darted under a large oak tree. Now the rain was coming down hard. They were close to the old Beemer house but needed to stay dry. They would get soaked if they looked around the yard.

"We should go to that bus shelter over there," said Andy. "It's safer than being under this tree."

Before the boys could move, they saw a bright flash. They covered their eyes. They heard a loud booming sound. They covered their ears. They felt the earth shake. They fell to the ground. "What's happening?" they both screamed.

When the boys looked up, they couldn't believe their eyes. Lightning had struck. The old Beemer house was on fire!

Chapter 3:
An Unexpected
Ride Home

. . . . .

Soon the flames were spreading through the house. The boys could feel the heat from where they were standing.

"What are we going to do?" asked Tom.

"I don't know," said Andy.

"Do you think the rain will put out the fire, Andy?"

"Not for a while," he answered. "Tom, we should call 911."

"That's exactly what we should do," Tom agreed. He pulled out his phone. He dialed 911. He waited for someone to answer but the screen on his phone went black. "Oh no," said Tom. "My battery just died."

Tom looked at the old Beemer place. Flames were shooting out the windows.

"Wait a minute. Do you hear that?" asked Andy. "I think it's a siren."

Andy was right. From the distance came the long low wail of a siren. Quiet at first. Then louder. They saw flashing lights on a red van. They heard a siren wailing. It was Mr. Ruby, the Fire Chief. He saw the two boys right away.

"Come on," he cried, "come over here."

The two boys dashed into the rain towards him. They rode their bikes as fast as they could. When they reached the Chief, they were soaked.

"Get into the van," he said, and ushered them in. He closed the door behind them. He plunked their bikes into the back. Just then a fire truck arrived, sirens blaring. The Chief barked orders to the driver. He pointed at the house, waving his arms from side to side. The driver of the fire truck nodded. Then the Chief came over.

"Where do you live?" he asked.

"Pleasant Avenue. Just down at the bottom of the hill," said Andy.

"The firefighters can handle this. I'll take you home. There's a lot of lightning out here. This is no place for you." With that, the Chief jumped behind the wheel. He started off down the hill.

"How did you know about the fire, Mr. Ruby?" asked Tom.

"The neighbours called 911, Tom. They saw the smoke from the house."

Tom looked over at Andy. He was glad the neighbour's phone worked fine.

"What about the musket?" Tom whispered. "If it was in the house, it will be ruined." Andy shrugged. It was too late. They couldn't do anything now.

The Chief pulled into Tom's driveway. Both Tom and the Chief stepped out of the van. Tom went to tell his parents he was home safe.

Mr. Ruby got his bike out of the van. Together, they put it in the garage. Tom waved goodbye. He went inside and Chief Ruby took Andy home.

Tom was glad to be out of the rain. But he was disappointed he hadn't had time to search Beemer's Hill. He felt there could be something there. After all, other people had found musket balls on the hill.

I've got to go back, he thought. *Maybe on the weekend Andy and I can try again.*

Chapter 4:
A Job

• • • • •

Tom was staring at the notice board outside the school library. Mrs. Willowby, the librarian, was advertising a job. It was to sort old newspapers. Tom thought it might be fun so he was going to apply.

"Hey kid, what are you doing?"

Tom looked up. It was Jason and his friend Kyle coming down the hall. They sneered at him.

"None of your business," said Tom. "Stay away from me."

"You know, Kyle," said Jason turning to his friend. "Little kids have so many problems. I hear they get caught in the rain sometimes. Isn't that right, Tom?"

"Hey, how did you . . . " Tom started to say, but then he stopped himself. "Just never mind. Go away," he said with his head hung low.

"Don't worry, kid. I went out last night and got you a birthday present. A new life jacket! Ha, ha, ha." Jason and Kyle were both laughing. They laughed all the way down the hall.

Mrs. Willowby stuck her head out the library door. "What's all the racket?"

"Oh nothing," mumbled Tom.

"Tom, can I help you?" asked Mrs. Willowby.

"I was wondering about the job. The one with the newspapers."

"I could certainly use the help," she said. "Are you interested?"

"Yes. I would like to try."

"Great. Let's start right now," she said.

"Now?" said Tom. "Really?"

The next thing he knew, Tom was in the back room of the library. "I've never been in here," he said. "What is this room?"

"It's called the Archives. This is where we keep all the old books and papers. Did you know we have newspapers going back seventy years?"

"Seventy years?" said Tom. "Wow."

"That's right," said Mrs. Willowby. "But they are all out of order. I've wanted to sort them out for years but never had the time. This year I'm going to do it. And you are going to help me."

"Ok, let's get started," exclaimed Tom.

Mrs. Willowby handed Tom a big stack of papers.

"Here, Tom. These are old city newspapers. I want you to sort them by date, from January through to December. There are more over there when you get this pile finished."

"I'll get right to it," said Tom.

He looked at the first newspaper. It was *The Maple Times*—the city newspaper. The date was March 1, 2000.

Wow, thought Tom. *This paper is over twenty years old*. But then he noticed something that made his jaw drop. Something that made his heart stop. Something that could be an important clue. It was the headline of the newspaper. He read the big, bold print.

"DISCOVERY OF 200-YEAR-OLD MUSKET BALLS PROVE A FAMOUS PIRATE LIVED ON BEEMER'S HILL."

Chapter 5:
The Legend

• • • • •

Tom grabbed the paper and started reading furiously.

Yesterday two local boys, James and Tyler, discovered musket balls on Beemer's Hill. Everyone in our city is talking about it.

"We were riding our bikes by the old orchard," said James. "I noticed something dark and round by some blueberry bushes. I bent down to pick it up, and it was heavy for something that small. I think it was made of lead."

"James called me over to take a look," said Tyler. "We both searched the area and found two other lead balls the same size. My dad told me they are musket balls. We gave them to the museum."

This amazing discovery proves what people have been saying for years. A famous pirate, named Black Eyed Bart, once lived on Beemer's Hill.

Wow, thought Tom as he looked up. *I knew Frank was right. A pirate did live here. I wonder what else it says.* He turned back to his reading.

"Black Eyed Bart moved to Beemer's Hill when he was old and stopped sailing," said Maple historian, Mr. Elder. "He had a party every full moon. You could hear the noise coming down into the valley. They laughed and joked and sang into the night. One night after a party there was a big fight. Someone who was hiding in the bushes shot at Black Eyed Bart. Most people think it was his greatest enemy, Jeffrey MacNay. Black Eyed Bart shot back with his musket, Boomer. These musket balls are proof of the fight, and proof that Black Eyed Bart lived there. These three musket balls came from his musket."

I never heard about these parties, thought Tom.

Black Eyed Bart disappeared after that fight. He was never seen again but some people think the hill is haunted and the parties are still happening.

"We have searched the hill for ghosts many times," said Police

Chief Garnet. "We have never found any. I don't think the hill is haunted, but the neighbours say they've heard strange sounds coming from Beemer's Hill."

I never heard anything about ghosts, thought Tom. *I will have to be careful if I go back there again.* Tom kept reading.

In our earliest records the pirate is called Black Bart, but in our later records he is called Black Eyed Bart.

"At first he was called Black Bart, because he had long, braided, black hair," said Mr. Elder. "He sailed the waters near Maple city in his ship called *Scallywag*, attacking other ships. One day Black Bart tried to rob a ship named *Blue Magic*. That ship's captain was Jeffrey MacNay. When Black Bart and his men jumped on board *Blue Magic*, a fight broke out. Jeffrey popped Black Bart right in the eye. The pirate screamed in pain. He called to his men, they jumped back onto *Scallywag*, and sailed away."

According to Mr. Elder, Jeffrey MacNay sailed after *Scallywag*, taunting the pirate by calling after him, "Your name is no longer Black Bart. From now on everyone will call you Black Eyed Bart." His men all laughed. "One day I will come after you," MacNay is reported to have said, "and when I find you, I will put a cannon ball right through your ship."

Black Eyed Bart, as the story goes, sailed off as fast as he could.

So, Jeffrey MacNay gave the pirate his name, Tom smiled as he thought about it. *He chased Black Eyed Bart away. He was a brave sailor.*

"Black Eyed Bart could never see well after the fight with Jeffrey MacNay," said Mrs. Fiddlebaum from the Maple Museum. "One day he got lucky. He found a monocle when he was hunting for treasure. He tried using it and could see again. After that he wore it everywhere. He named it Searcher, and it was his favourite thing. He also had a beautiful musket he called Boomer, but no one has ever found it. We would love to have Boomer in our museum."

I wonder what happened to his musket, thought Tom. *It must be out there somewhere. I have to find it.*

"How is it going?" asked Mrs. Willowby as she poked her head into the Archive room.

"Oh . . . uh . . . " stumbled Tom. "Fine. It's going fine."

"You sure?"

"Yes. Sure. I was just . . . getting the hang of it," he replied.

"Ok. If you need any help you can call me." Mrs. Willowby left the room.

Tom was excited. He had a new job. The best job a boy could ever have. And now he knew more about Black Eyed Bart. Tom knew he had to get back to Beemer's Hill. Tomorrow was Saturday. He'd have all day to hunt for Boomer!

Chapter 6:
The Barn

• • • • •

Tom and Andy looked around. They couldn't believe it. Almost a week ago they'd been up here on the hill. They'd stopped under the oak tree while the rain poured down. The Fire Chief had rescued them and taken them home. And, most importantly, the Beemer house had been here. Now everything was different.

"What happened?" asked Tom.

"I don't know," said Andy. "I heard they were clearing the land. After the fire they took the rubble out of here. They wanted to make it safe. I had no idea they did this. The house . . . it's gone."

"Everything's gone," grumbled Tom. "The house, the walls, the floors. It's all gone."

"Just some stones where the house used to sit," said Andy. "They were part of the foundation. What do we do now?"

Tom shrugged. "I don't know. There's nothing here now." He slumped to the ground. He'd come to Beemer's Hill to find Black Eyed Bart's musket. He'd thought for sure he'd be able to find it today. Now his dream had gone up in flames.

"Let's look around," said Andy. Then a big grin came across his face. "Race you through those trees over there."

"You're on," said Tom, jumping to his feet.

Both boys ran to their bikes. Andy got there first.

"No fair," said Tom.

"Can't catch me," said Andy. And off he went.

Tom raced to catch up but it was too late. Andy was too far ahead. Tom did the best he could anyway. The boys bounced over the rough ground. They scooted under low branches. Tom was still behind when they came into a clearing.

"I won," yelled Andy.

Tom slammed on the brakes. He looked up and his eyes opened wide. He looked past Andy into the distance.

"What?" said Andy.

"That," said Tom. "What's that?"

On the other side of the clearing stood a rickety shack. The wood was old. The roof had holes in it. The door hung crookedly on one hinge.

"It's an old shed. Or maybe a small barn," said Andy. "So what?"

"So everything," said Tom. "Do you realize what this means?"

"What?"

"The musket—it could be in there." Tom pointed.

"Do you think so?" asked Andy.

"You bet I do. Come on. Let's go inside."

"It doesn't look too safe," said Andy. "Maybe we should be careful."

"This is it. I can feel it. Andy, you keep watch outside. I'm going in."

Chapter 7:
The Loft

• • • • •

Tom stood in the doorway of the barn while Andy waited outside. The door swung loosely on its hinge. He peered ahead.

It looks bigger inside, he thought. *At least the holes in the roof let a little light in.*

He crept forward, one slow step at a time. The floor groaned under his feet. Tom looked down. The floor was old but still strong. He took a few more steps. He

heard the wind blow outside. He thought he heard voices.

Oh no, he thought. *Ghosts. There really are strange noises up here!* He turned to go back. Just then the door blew shut. Tom jumped as it slammed. He was caught inside.

The voices got louder. He could hear them coming closer. They were after him. Tom started to panic. What could he do?

I have to hide, he thought. *Where can I hide?*

Tom looked around. He saw old wooden planks beside him. They were nailed into the wall and formed a ladder. Tom saw a loft at the top of the barn.

I have to go up, he thought. *I can hide in the loft*.

The voices were louder now. He could hear them right outside. He thought about Andy alone out there. He was sure Andy could get away. After all, Andy could ride fast.

Tom tested the first rung. It groaned under his weight but held him. He scampered up the ladder. He jumped into the loft just in time. Tom heard a voice speak outside.

"Hey, Andy, what are you doing here? Are you lost? Ha, ha, ha."

Wait a minute, thought Tom. *I know that voice.*

"Where's your goofy friend? Isn't that his bike? The little kid must be around here somewhere."

Oh no, thought Tom. *It's Jason. I'll bet Kyle is out there too. I can't let them find me in here.*

Tom nestled deeper into the loft. There was straw up there. Old straw. Old musty straw and it smelled awful. He looked around. Tucked into the back corner was a bird's nest. Tom hoped there were no birds there now. The last thing he needed was a bird attack. Tom heard the voices coming closer.

"What's in the barn? Is your little friend in here, Andy? What do you say we give him a scare?" And with that the door burst open and in came Jason.

"BOOO!" He screamed.

Tom knew it was only Jason, not a ghost, but it still scared him. He edged farther into the loft.

"Where are you, kid? Come out, wherever you are. What's the matter, are you scared?"

Jason looked around the barn. He went to the far end. He poked around the floor. He came back to the front. Then he stopped and looked up.

"What's this, Kyle?" he said. "A ladder. Hmmm." Jason tested the first rung. "I wonder how strong this is?" he said. He jumped up and down on it with both feet. It broke!

"Ahhh," he screamed as he fell to the ground.

Up in the loft, Tom muffled a laugh.

"This rickety old thing can't hold me up," Jason grumbled. "That kid could never be up there. Come on Kyle, let's get out of here." He walked out the door, snarling.

Tom didn't move for a long time. Finally, he turned his head. He couldn't hear anything. He looked around the loft. He saw the bird's nest. There didn't seem to be any birds in there, but something twinkled. Tom looked closer. Light came through a hole in the roof and sparkled when it hit the bird's nest.

What is that? Tom thought excitedly. *There's something there.*

He reached over. He touched the nest. Something was buried inside it. He thought it looked like a jewel. Tom dug at it with his fingers. He pushed. He pulled. Finally, he wrestled it free.

He held in his hands a small object. He dusted it off and held it up. It was round. It was very smooth. He wondered what it was.

Just then he heard footsteps and the door slammed shut. Tom jumped. And when he did the small round object fell from his hands to the floor below.

Chapter 8:
Diamonds or Glasses

• • • • •

Tom was up in the loft. Then he heard Andy's voice below.

"Are you ok up there?" It was Andy who had entered the shack.

"You scared me," said Tom. "I dropped something. We've got to find it." Andy looked frantically over the ground. He couldn't find anything. There was just dirt and bits of straw scattered on the floor. "What am I looking for?" he asked.

"I don't know," said Tom, "but it belonged to Black Eyed Bart."

Tom scooted down the ladder, jumping over the last step. He landed with a thud. He rushed over to help Andy. Then Andy found something.

"I've got it," exclaimed Andy. He held it up. "I wonder what it is?" he said thoughtfully.

Tom was excited. "Do you think it's a diamond, Andy?"

"No. It looks like glass," said Andy. "You know what, Tom? I think it's a lens. It fell out of someone's glasses."

Tom was stunned. "Glasses? That's no good. I want a diamond." Tom frowned. He was not happy. "Well I don't care what it is. I still think it belonged to Black Eyed Bart."

"What do we know about Black Eyed Bart?" asked Andy. "Let's review."

"Ok," said Tom. "He was a pirate. He sailed a ship called *Scallywag*. He owned a musket named Boomer. And he wore a monocle—whatever that is. It was called Searcher. It helped him see better."

Andy's eyes flew open wide. "A monocle?" he exclaimed. "Black Eyed Bart owned a monocle?"

"Why, yes," said Tom.

"This could be it," shouted Andy. He was now jumping up and down. "A monocle is a glass lens. People used to wear them before glasses were invented."

Andy handed the monocle to Tom. "Here, hold it up to your eye,"

First it needed cleaning. Tom sank the monocle into his shirt. He rubbed it gently to clean it. He checked it over. It was nice and clear now. Slowly, he held it up to the light.

"Wow, it looks like a magnifying glass," Tom said. He moved the monocle towards his eye. He held it in place and looked down.

"It is a magnifying glass," he shouted. "The ground looks a lot closer."

He went outside and looked at the trees. They looked closer too. Everything looked bigger with the monocle. Tom cheered loudly. "We found it. We found Searcher. How much do you think it's worth, Andy?"

"I'm not sure," Andy replied. "You know, Tom, we might have a problem. How do we know it was Bart's monocle?"

"It must be his," said Tom.

"But we have to prove it," said Andy.

"Let's look around, then. Maybe Searcher can help us find something else." And with that, Tom started to search the whole clearing.

The two boys spent over an hour searching. They used the monocle to look closely over the ground. They found nothing. Tom was getting impatient. Andy was getting bored.

Finally, Andy spoke. "There's nothing here, Tom. Let's go home."

"There must be something," said Tom. "Let's keep looking."

"I'm hungry," said Andy. "It's lunch time. Let's go home and think about it."

"Ok," answered Tom reluctantly. "But we have to come back later."

"Deal," agreed Andy. "Race you home."

The two boys ran for their bikes.

Once again, Andy got to his bike first. Once again, he got ahead of Tom. And once again, Andy won the race.

Chapter 9:
The Red Spot

• • • • •

Later that afternoon, the boys returned to Beemer's Hill.

Andy looked over the area where the house used to stand. "There's nothing here, Tom," he said. "Let's go riding somewhere else."

"Wait," said Tom. "We never used Searcher here. Give me a few minutes, and then we can go."

Tom stepped down from his bike. He put the monocle up to his eye. Slowly he moved forward, scanning the ground.

Tom was just about to quit when he noticed something. The ground looked funny. One spot had a red glow on it. At first he thought he'd imagined it. He looked again. There it was!

"What is that?" Tom said, pointing. He was very excited now.

"What are you pointing at?" asked Andy. "I don't see anything."

"Over there. That red spot," said Tom pointing again.

"I still don't see anything. You've lost your mind," said Andy. He grinned his big grin. "Searcher has made you crazy." He laughed.

"No it hasn't." Tom ran over to the spot. "It's right here," he said, touching the ground. "Look for yourself."

Andy came over and took the monocle from Tom. He placed it up to his eye. Andy looked down at the ground. His mouth flew open wide.

"It *is* a red spot," he exclaimed. "Something is buried here."

Tom and Andy knew what to do. They needed to dig a hole where the red spot was. Andy was worried because they had no shovel. Tom, however, was ready. He'd brought a small garden shovel from home. It was strapped to the back of his bike.

"I'll get my shovel. Then we can start digging," he said.

Tom returned with the shovel. The boys took turns digging in the dirt. Then they heard a sound.

Clank.

"What was that?" asked Andy.

"I hit something with the shovel," said Tom. He started digging faster. Soon he could see something black. A metal object was buried in the dirt.

Andy reached down to help. Both boys grabbed hold and pulled. They pulled hard.

They pulled even harder. Then the object came out of the ground. It was an old shotgun!

"Look, it's a musket," said Tom proudly. He held it up high.

"It's a beauty," said Andy. "I can't believe we found it."

"It's Black Eyed Bart's musket!" Tom started to hoot and holler with excitement.

Andy joined in. He was excited too.

"This is a great find," said Tom. "I wonder if there's more here."

"Let's take this home first," said Andy. We can get supper. Then we can come back tomorrow. Maybe we can find more pirate loot."

Tom agreed. By now he was hungry too. Hunting for pirate loot was tough work. They had been busy all day.

The boys raced down the hill. They raced down Pleasant Avenue. They raced into Andy's driveway. Guess who got there first? Andy did.

Tom took the musket over to his place. He showed his parents and his brother, Frank. They were excited too. The musket was a great treasure.

"You will be famous at school," said Frank, beaming. He gave his brother a pat on the shoulder. "You've done great work, Tom. I'm proud of you. Everyone at school will be, too."

Tom smiled. He really liked what Frank said.

"But it's not a toy," said Frank. "Don't play with it."

"I know," said Tom. "I'm going to donate it to the museum."

"Great idea," said Frank. "It belongs there."

"I'm starving," said Tom. "Let's eat."

Tom was so hungry he ate three hot dogs.

The next day, Tom and Andy went back to the old Beemer property. They searched all afternoon. Sadly, they found nothing else. Tom wasn't discouraged, though. They had already found something special.

"When are you going to donate the musket?" asked Andy.

"As soon as I can. Mrs. Fiddlebaum will be very happy to have it. They've wanted it for a long time. But I'm keeping Searcher. Maybe it will come in handy another time."

"Great idea," said Andy. "Maybe you can get your picture in the paper."

And that's exactly what happened.

Tom and Andy Find Musket

Pet Squirrel Missing

Chapter 10:
The Chase

• • • • •

The next few days were great fun for Tom and Andy. They met Mrs. Fiddlebaum, who ran the museum. They were her guests for a day. They posed for pictures in the newspaper, *The Maple Times*. And they donated the musket to the museum. Mrs. Fiddlebaum said the musket was 200 years old. It was now a prize piece in the museum.

But that wasn't all. Below the musket was a card. The card said, "The museum is grateful to Tom and Andy. They donated this fine musket. It is 200 years old."

But there was still one more thing. Both Tom and Andy got a one-year pass to the museum. They could visit any time they wished. For free.

The whole town was happy. Everyone was excited. They all thought Tom and Andy had done something special.

Everyone, that is, except for Jason.

The next day, Tom was at school. The students all congratulated him. When the day was over, he went to get his bike. As he walked towards it, he heard someone yelling behind him.

"There he is. It's that little kid. The one who thinks he's so good."

Tom turned around. It was Jason. Kyle was with him. Both boys were running towards him.

Tom bolted for his bike.

The museum is grateful
to Tom and Andy.
They donated this fine musket.
It is 200 years old.

"Let's catch him," yelled Jason.

Tom ran as fast as he could. He hoped he could reach his bike before Jason caught him.

Jason was closing in fast. "Look out kid," he yelled, "I'm the ghost of Black Eyed Bart, ha, ha, ha."

Finally, Tom reached his bike. Jason was right behind him. Then Tom saw a problem. *Oh no*, he thought. *My bike is locked. I can't escape. I'll have to stand up to him.* Tom spun around to face Jason.

"I'm not scared of you, Jason," he said firmly. "Why don't you just leave me alone?"

Jason stopped in his tracks. He was surprised that Tom hadn't run away. Before Jason could say or do anything, Tom heard a familiar voice,

"Hey Jason, what are you doing?"

Tom turned. So did Jason. It was Frank, Tom's older brother. Frank was two years older than Jason.

"You forgot to congratulate Tom today," Frank said to Jason. "I think now is a good time to do that."

Jason's face turned beet red. He hadn't expected to see Frank. "Oh yeah . . . that's just what I was going to do," he said. He turned to Tom. "That musket looks great in the museum. Nice job finding it."

"That's great," said Frank. "Now we can all go home happy. Can't we?"

"Right on," said Tom, and he flashed his brother a big smile.

"Let's go home," said Frank.

"Not yet," said Tom. "I want to go to the museum. I'm meeting Andy there. There's something cool that I want to show him."

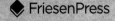

FriesenPress

One Printers Way
Altona, MB R0G 0B0
Canada

www.friesenpress.com

Copyright © 2022 by Edward Penner
First Edition — 2022

All rights reserved.

The characters and events in this story are purely fictional and should be enjoyed as such. Grand adventures are always fun to read about, but wherever you go always remember to play safe, and let your parents know where you are.

Illustrated by Paul Schultz

ISBN
978-1-03-912940-5(Hardcover)
978-1-03-912939-9 (Paperback)
978-1-03-912941-2 (eBook)

1. JUVENILE FICTION, ACTION & ADVENTURE, PIRATES

Distributed to the trade by The Ingram Book Company

Coming Soon!

* * * * * *

The Legend of Black Eyed Bart
Book 2

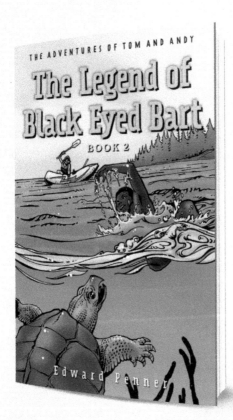

CPSIA information can be obtained
at www.ICGtesting.com
Printed in the USA
BVHW092023070522
636321BV00003B/7

9 781039 129399